CHAPTER 1
Monday

Dear Mum,

I hope you get this letter. I'm putting it in a bottle and throwing it in the sea. Toothy Tim says that's the way to send letters when you're a pirate.

Toothy is the ship's cook, but I don't think he's very good at it. The crew are always moaning about burnt potatoes. I'm cook's boy, so I'm meant to help him, but I'm not very good either.

I thought the salt was sugar, and everyone was nearly sick after they ate our apple pie. We had to sneak them buckets of grog because they were all so thirsty.

Race Further with Reading

The Petrified Pirate

By Vivian French

Illustrated by Mike Phillips

W
FRANKLIN WATTS
LONDON • SYDNEY

I know you didn't want me to go to sea, Mum, but I'll be back soon ... and I'll bring loads of gold with me. We're going to find treasure! And when I get back I'll buy a cow and some chickens, and you won't have to go out to work ever again.

The *Sulky Skull* is dirty and very messy. The crew are dirty and messy, and Captain Blackbeard is the dirtiest and messiest of all. His beard is ENORMOUS, and it's got grubby ribbons and bits of rope and old string tied in it.

The crew are very proud of the captain, because he won a competition for Best Beard. He beat seventeen other pirate captains! And what did he win? A treasure map! So I'm definitely going to be rich.

Guess what, Mum? We're going to sail to Dragon's Head Island. When we get there, we have to find three tall palm trees in a line, and then walk a hundred paces north. That's where the treasure is hidden. I found out when Toothy sent me to the captain's cabin with a mug of grog.

The captain had a map on his table. I told him it was upside down and he growled at me. "Think you're so clever, don't you! Bet you can't read them there instructions out loud!" So I did. He told me I was a slimy slug of a boy, and if I caused any trouble he'd feed me to the sharks.

Did I tell you Toothy has a pet monkey? He's called Bubbles. Captain Blackbeard doesn't like him much, so Toothy keeps him hidden out of sight. Bubbles likes me. I flick peanuts at him and he catches them and eats them! Sometimes he flicks them back – but I'm not as good at catching them as he is.

Toothy says there's a storm coming, so I'd better stop for now.

CHAPTER 2
Saturday

It was a wild storm. We had to tie everything down in case it got washed overboard, but nobody tied up Toothy's food barrels. They fell over and the pickled cabbage barrel split. Everything smells cabbagey now.

Bubbles doesn't like the smell at all. He keeps sneaking off. On Thursday I found him asleep in Mouldy Jack's hammock.

The day before that he was stuffing fish bait into one of Nobbly Norm's socks. Luckily, Nobbly didn't notice. Toothy says dirty socks are the best, because the dirt keeps your toes warm.

But Mum – today something DREADFUL happened! I feel terrible! Bubbles went missing while Toothy was cooking breakfast, and I couldn't find him anywhere.

While Toothy was busy dishing out burnt ship's biscuit and half-cooked eggs, I went to look on the other decks.

I found Bubbles in the captain's cabin – and he had torn a hole in the treasure map! I folded the map so the torn bit didn't show and stuffed Bubbles inside my jacket.

I dashed back to the galley and WHACK!

I ran straight into Captain Blackbeard.

"Ha! If it isn't the mimsy wimsy wash pot,"

he said, and he scowled a horrible scowl.

"Sneaking around where you don't belong!

And WHAT are you hiding?"

Next minute he saw Bubbles' tail and he snarled.

"What's this? You're here to work, boy, WORK!" And then – Mum, it was TERRIBLE! He threw Bubbles and my jacket overboard. I heard Bubbles yell, and there was a splash ... and then silence.

Toothy is VERY sad, but he says it wasn't my fault. I wish I could make it up to him. When we find treasure I'll give him half my share. You won't mind, will you?

Last night, some of the bacon disappeared and so did a bowl of cold potatoes. Toothy thinks there's a ghost. I don't think ghosts eat bacon and potatoes.

Toothy is CERTAIN there's a ghost. Bubbles's bag of peanuts has gone missing, and a box of ship's biscuits. I've started jumping at strange noises too. I'm really scared about what will happen when the captain finds the hole in his treasure map ... I wake up in the night with my stomach tied in horrible knots. I'm SO SCARED!

CHAPTER 3
Monday

It's happened. Captain Blackbeard found the hole. He came storming down this morning, booming:

"Boiling bloaters! Where's that horrible worm? I'm going to make him walk the plank! He's a weaselly wart, a scab, a blot, and a disgrace to the *Sulky Skull*!"

Then he dragged me up on deck.

"This worm tore holes in our treasure map!"

he yelled. The crew booed and hissed at me.

"Haul out the plank!" Blackbeard bellowed.

Mouldy Jack grinned an evil grin.

"My pleasure, Captain!"

Mum ... I was PETRIFIED!

When Mouldy Jack came stomping back my legs went wobbly with fright. Then – PING! Something flew though the air and hit the captain on the nose! It rattled on the deck and I saw it was a peanut.

"OUCH!" The captain let go of me and I RAN!

I sprinted across the deck and flung myself up the mast. I climbed and climbed until I was right at the top. I wriggled into the crow's nest, and my heart was thumping as if it was about to burst as I peeped over the edge.

I thought the captain would be coming after me, but he wasn't. He was picking himself up off the deck, and shouting at Toothy Tim.

"You crumbling cuttlefish! You bristle-nose barracuda! Trying to save that swab of a boy, were you? You tripped me up!"

"I never!" Toothy was bright red. "I never tripped you Captain!"

"I'll have YOU walk the plank, Toothy Tim!" Captain Blackbeard waved his cutlass and charged at Toothy – and a long hairy arm came out from under a heap of old sails, and DOWN crashed the captain again!

Had I really seen an arm? I looked again
and there was nothing except a few peanut
shells ... but then something on the horizon
caught my eye. An island! In the shape of
a dragon's head! I took a deep breath.
"LAND HO!" I yelled.

There was a roar from the crew. The captain struggled to his feet, fishing in his pocket for his telescope.

"Hoist the mainsail! Treasure in sight!" Mouldy Jack jumped to the wheel, and six of the crew leapt into the rigging.

While nobody was looking I slithered down. As I reached the deck Toothy grabbed me. "Thought you was going to be swimming, Joe." I didn't answer. I was staring at the heap of old sails. An eye was peering out and I knew who it was ... Bubbles! Then he hid back under the sails again.

CHAPTER 4
Tuesday

The *Sulky Skull* reached Dragon's Head Island just as the sun was setting.

"Every man to be on deck at dawn!" Blackbeard ordered, and we were. He was waiting for us, growling impatiently.

"Shake a leg, you scurvy lot! Lower the jolly boat!"

As soon as the jolly boat was in the water, the captain climbed in and Mouldy Jack and Nobbly Norm followed him. Then he ordered me to come too, and Toothy Tim as well.

Mouldy started sniggering when we got in. "Fancy! You two are going to have a nice long holiday ... hope you like coconuts!" Nobbly cackled loudly. "A cook who can't cook, and a boy who tears up treasure maps! We'll be well rid of you two ..."

My stomach tied itself into knots again and I could hardly breathe.

"But you can't ..." I began.

"Oh yes we can!" Captain Blackbeard grinned a black-toothed grin, and he held up a canvas bag that was wriggling madly. "You and your monkey! You can all climb trees together!"

Toothy leant towards me as we were rowed towards the island. "I'm scared, Joe!"

"Me too," I whispered back. "I'm petrified!" And I was.

The three tall palm trees were near the beach, and the pirates grew more and more excited as we walked a hundred paces north. Mouldy Jack and Nobbly Norm had spades, and they began to dig furiously.

THUNK! Nobbly's spade hit something solid.
A moment later Mouldy Jack grunted –
"It's a treasure chest!" Captain Blackbeard
rubbed his hands, smiling a greedy smile.
"Time to count the gold, boys! Let's see what
we've got." He opened the chest ...

... but there was no treasure, just a roll of paper. Mouldy Jack growled.

"You've been tricked, Cap'n! That competition you won ... they've robbed you rotten!"

"Ah ..." Captain Blackbeard shut one eye and squinted at the crooked writing. "Never did have much to do with that ABC stuff," he said. He grabbed me, and shoved the paper under my nose. "Here! You read it!"

CHAPTER 5
Tuesday continued

And that was when I realised Captain
Blackbeard couldn't read! My mind started
whirling as I began the letter.

"Greetings, Blackbeard, you mouldy old bag
of bones!" There was a gasp and Captain
Blackbeard went purple.

"You can't read, and nor can your beetle-brained crew. So you'll never find the treasure – ha, ha, ha! But I'm a man of my word, Blackbeard, and you won the competition fair and square. So here's where to look –" I stopped.

"Get on with it!" The captain glared at me.

"If I read the rest," I said slowly, "will you let me and Toothy come back to the *Sulky Skull* and share the treasure?"

"Yes, yes, YES! Whatever you want!" Blackbeard nodded his head furiously. "Word of honour as a pirate," he promised.

"Right," I said, pretending I was studying the writing. "I've got it! Go a hundred and fifty paces south, then forty paces west. Then dig. And good luck be with you!"

Mouldy Jack and Nobbly Norm set off at a run, and Captain Blackbeard followed them, panting.

"QUICK!" I said to Toothy. "That's not what the letter said! The treasure's right here! We've got to find it before they realise they've been tricked!"

I jumped down into the hole the pirates had dug. I tapped the chest, then began feeling round the edges of the lid. SNAP!

A piece of wood slid to one side ...
and out tumbled a rush of gold coins.
"Oh!" I rubbed my eyes ... but the treasure
was real. Toothy's mouth dropped open so
wide he looked like a goldfish.

We stuffed our pockets full, and we filled the canvas bag that Bubbles had been shoved in ... and then we ran down the beach, Bubbles jumping beside us. We leapt into the jolly boat, and Toothy took the oars. "Time to go home!" I said. "Hurrah!"

p.s. – The pirates didn't realise we'd gone until they'd dug the most enormous hole. When they finally looked up, they went absolutely mad. Captain Blackbeard shouted something that sounded like "ARRRRRRRR!" but we couldn't really hear. Then he waded into the sea ...

... and that was when the shark appeared! The captain just about made it back to the shore, and even though we were a long way away I could see he was shaking all over. Mouldy Jack and Nobbly Norm were very, very pale.

"Perfect picture to see those three sitting together like that." Toothy grinned. "What was that word you used, Joe? The one that means scared?"

"Petrified?" I said. Toothy nodded.

"That's the one. Petrified pirates, that's what they be!"

So that was the way I got rich, Mum.

Toothy and I will be back very soon ...

so put the kettle on. And could you please

buy some peanuts for Bubbles?

Love,

Joe.

Franklin Watts
First published in Great Britain in 2016 by
The Watts Publishing Group

ISBN 978 1 4451 4987 5 (hbk)
ISBN 978 1 4451 4986 8 (pbk)
ISBN 978 1 4451 4985 1 (library ebook)

Franklin Watts
An imprint of
Hachette Children's Group
Part of The Watts Publishing Group
Carmelite House
50 Victoria Embankment
London EC4Y 0DZ

An Hachette UK Company
www.hachette.co.uk

www.franklinwatts.co.uk

Series Editor: Melanie Palmer
Series Advisor: Catherine Glavina
Cover Designer: Cathryn Gilbert
Design Manager: Peter Scoulding